The
Summer
We Found
the Baby

The
Summer
We Found
the Baby

AMY HEST

CANDLEWICK PRESS

Copyright © 2020 by Amy Hest
Chapter opener illustrations copyright
© 2020 by Jamey Christoph

First edition 2020

Library of Congress Catalog Card Number pending
ISBN 978-0-7636-6007-9

20 21 22 23 24 25 LBM 10 9 8 7 6 5 4 3 2 1

Printed in Melrose Park, IL, U.S.A.

This book was typeset in Vollkorn.

Candlewick Press
99 Dover Street
Somerville, Massachusetts 02144

visit us at www.candlewick.com

For Nancy and Erica, forever

1.

THE
BABY

Julie Sweet

age 11

I'm the one who found her. A real, live baby girl and I saw her first. I saw the basket. Right over there, on the steps of the new children's library. A tiny little baby! All by herself in that basket! She was so brave, though. She wasn't even crying.

I just wanted to hold her awhile. I didn't mean to take the baby.

Martha Sweet
age 6

You know what I thought? I thought it was a doll! And I don't even like dolls! Then something happened. Which is this. It *moved.* And made a *gurgle-a-gurgle-a* sound. HELP! I screamed. HELP! Then Julie was holding it and their noses were touching and you know what else? There was a little green pig inside the basket. HERE'S YOUR NICE PIG, I said. LOOK AT PIGGY DANCING! The baby only looked at Julie. She didn't love her pig — oh, poor little pig — so I put it in my pocket for a while.

Bruno Ben-Eli

age 12

It was August 31, that's when everything happened. That morning, while they were working, I wrote my parents a goodbye note. It was my first time writing a goodbye note, but I like what I wrote. I like how it shows my thoughtful side. Here are my exact words.

Dear Mom and Dear Dad,

I have to go somewhere immediately but not forever. Can't say more, sorry.
Your son, Bruno

P.S. Don't worry, I'm not running
away from home. I would never do
that, don't worry.

See what I mean? Thoughtful. I left it on my pillow, along with a nice little picture of me for my parents to look at. Then, at exactly 7:45 a.m., I was ready to leave. So I left.

My house is right on the beach, and you can walk on the beach all the way to town if you want. It's a pretty long walk, but I had plenty of time. I knew I had plenty of time because I kept checking my watch. Which is not in actual fact *my* watch, but I wear it every day. Ben said I could. Ben. That's my brother. Private Benjamin Ben-Eli, bravest soldier in the war. BRUNO, CATCH! That's what he called from the train that day — his leaving day — and the train whistle blew and his watch came sailing out the window, and the train pulled out, and then he was gone. Gone to war.

Before the war, I never wrote a letter to Ben. Now I write one a week. My mother's idea, not mine, but I don't mind. Mostly I think up funny jokes to stick in my letters to Ben. In case he's sad over there. Even brave soldiers are sad sometimes. My father told me that.

You know what's the best day? A day when there's a letter from Ben. And that morning I had one in my pocket, a top-secret letter, just to me, not my parents and me. *I know I can count on you, Bruno.* That's what he wrote, and that's why I was going away. Seventy miles away. To New York City. I had to find someone there — somewhere in the city — and give her a message from Ben. It would be my first time alone on the train. My first time alone in the city. A lot of kids would be scared. Not me. Ben was counting on me. I couldn't be scared. And I couldn't stop thinking about the secret he told me in that letter. It was huge.

The train station is on Front Street. So is the library. Which is where I saw the basket. High up, near the door. Then I saw Julie Sweet, in all her unfriendly glory, and she was holding this *baby*, of all things, and no one else was around. Not one single person. Unless you count Martha. That's Julie's little sister, and the minute she saw me, she was waving her arms in a way that meant: *Bruno, Bruno! Come on up!* I shook my head: *Not possible, not now, I have to go somewhere.* But Martha kept at it: *Look, Bruno, look! We found this little baby!*

It's a good thing I changed my mind. Because I'm the one who saw the envelope that came in the basket with the baby.

Please open immediately. Instructions inside. That's what it said on the envelope. *Open immediately? Instructions inside?* I picked up the envelope. Obviously, my services were needed.

2.

LEAVING THE SCENE

Julie

It's true. I loved her. I loved everything about her. Kissing her cheek. Rubbing my nose on her soft little neck. And the smell of her, that baby smell. I loved that, too. Then *Bruno,* of all people, showed up, with his stupid comments (WOW, IT'S *BALD*), stupid advice (BETTER NOT DROP IT), and stupid question (WHAT ARE YOU GOING TO DO WITH IT?). *What are you going to do with it?* As soon as those words blew out of his mouth, I knew what I had to do. So I put the baby in the basket, picked up the basket, and left.

Martha

All my life I wanted a baby sister and now she was finally here! JULIE, JULIE! I said. LET'S CALL HER NANCY AND LET'S TAKE HER HOME! But Julie was bossy and *shush*-ing me. TOO MUCH *TALKING*, MARTHA, WE HAVE TO *GO*, MARTHA, FOLLOW *ME*, MARTHA. Then we were running away from the library! With my baby sister, Nancy!

Bruno

Usually I don't even care that much about babies. But this was different. This one came in an actual basket. With actual instructions. Like some *mystery* you see in the movies, one I could easily solve in ten minutes flat. Only I didn't have ten minutes. Or even two, the reason being Julie. The same Julie who hadn't said a single word to me in sixteen days, all of a sudden she's *leaving the scene*. And here's the kicker—she's doing it with the baby. I repeat, with the baby. *Holy everything,* I thought, *Julie Sweet is a kidnapper.* She was really moving, too. Away from the library. Step after step and without looking back. Now crossing Front Street. Now turning into Gary Lane, this short little street that stops at the beach. *The beach!* I thought. *She's going to the beach!*

Once last summer, the summer he enlisted, I followed Ben somewhere. I feel kind of bad about that now. About following Ben that time. Maybe I'll tell him. After the war, when he comes home, I'll tell him then. He won't be too mad. Ben is never too mad. Julie's the opposite of Ben. Do one little thing *she* doesn't like and she's mad at you for the rest of your life. Who knows, maybe that's just what girls do.

I stuffed the envelope in my pocket, crouched low, and kept out of sight. I moved left, right, left. Ducked low. And followed her onto the foggy beach.

3.

YOU NEED A PLAN

Julie

To tell you the truth, I don't even *like* to cook. But that morning I got out of bed on the dot of six, all because I had this plan to bake a cake. A very *important* cake. For a very *important* person. It was my first time baking a cake, but I wasn't too worried. When I got to the hard parts, such as *beating the egg whites until they stand up in peaks,* I just kept telling myself *keep calm and concentrate.* Then Martha woke up and it was nonstop I WANT TO HELP! YOU NEVER LET ME HELP! I WANT TO STIR BATTER! YOU NEVER LET ME STIR BATTER! Finally, a long time later, there was cake. *Pink clouds on angel food cake.* Did it look like the beautiful picture in the magazine? Honestly, it did not. Thanks to a certain dog in my life. *Warning: Never trust your dog around a cake.* I rescued most of it, though, and took it all the way to town, to the library. I took it in my wagon. Exactly the way I'd planned it.

But then she was there, at the top of the steps.

Maybe some things just *happen* and there is no plan for what happens next. You are five years old and there's a new baby in the house — WE'LL CALL HER MARTHA, says Pop. A new baby sister but no mother in the house — THEIR MOMMY DIED, someone whispers, IMPOSSIBLY SAD, they say. You cry with Pop. You cry alone. But somehow you go to kindergarten every day. And brush your teeth every day, and attend story hour at the New York Public

Library. The baby wails in the night. You run to her crib and pat her head. HERE I AM, MARTHA! SISTER JULIE IS HERE! You cry with Pop. You cry alone. But somehow chocolate ice cream still tastes like chocolate ice cream. And skating is still skating, under the stars in Central Park. Martha? Well, she's six now, and you sleep in twin beds, but she climbs into yours quite often. TELL ME A STORY, STARRING MOMMY, she says. No plan, but you talk about a soft pink bathrobe and silver-dollar pancakes on Sundays, and you both fall asleep, nose-to-nose, on your pillow.

Martha

Julie *promised.* She promised George. Like this: OF COURSE YOU CAN COME WITH US, GEORGE. THE LIBRARY PARTY IS FOR *EVERYONE,* EVEN DOGS. But that was before he ate Julie's cake. Not the *whole* cake, George would never do that. Just one bite. NOBODY WILL NOTICE. IT'S SUCH A PRETTY CAKE! WE CAN EVEN PATCH IT IF YOU WANT. I AM REALLY GOOD AT PATCHING! That's what I told Julie, and I tried to smooth the cake. Only Julie didn't care about that. All she cared about was being mad. Julie being mad: BAD DOG, YOU ATE MY CAKE! NO PARTY FOR YOU! BAD DOGS STAY HOME! George hates when someone's mad at him. I never get mad at George. And I never break a promise.

We walked to town. Julie was grumpy. *And* she walked too fast. *And* she wouldn't let me pull the wagon. Or sit in the wagon with the cake. *And* she made me wear shoes because IT'S A *PARTY*, MARTHA. EVERYONE WEARS SHOES TO A PARTY.

I know who made a hole in Julie's cake. Which wasn't George. I only meant to *smell* it, maybe *lick* it, but then I was sticking my finger in Julie's cake and it was the best thing you ever want to eat! But then I got scared about what if Julie finds out, so I ran upstairs to put on my dress and my pretty red shoes for the party.

I was going to tell Julie about who

didn't eat the cake, but then we found the baby and Julie forgot to be mad at George. Oh, and you know what else she forgot? The cake! She left it at the library, in my wagon!

Bruno

You know the type: never does anything *wrong*, always does everything *right*. That's Julie Sweet for you, and that's why stealing a baby made no sense. She wasn't the type. *Go back to library! Take it back now,* I thought, *before you get caught! Take back the baby!* But Julie, being Julie — translation: *annoying* — just kept going. The responsible side of my brain was saying things like *kidnapping is a criminal act . . . better keep an eye on that baby.* So I did the responsible thing: I stayed back but not too far back. I ran when they ran, Julie and Martha, in and out of the fog. I stopped when they stopped and kept out of sight. You could hear them, though, and you could practically predict what they would say, kind of like this: First Julie says something along the lines of COME ON, MARTHA, HURRY! Then Martha says something like I WANT TO HOLD THE BABY! Then Julie goes: *I* HOLD THE BABY, ONLY *ME*. And Martha goes: YOU *ALWAYS* HAVE FUN AND I *NEVER* HAVE FUN! Like I said, pretty predictable. But when Julie said, WE HAVE A LONG WAY TO GO, MARTHA, ARE YOU COMING OR NOT, that's when it hit me. Where Julie was taking the baby. She was taking it to Camp Mitchel.

4.

CAMP
MITCHEL

Julie

If the subject is Bruno Ben-Eli, sorry, no compliments. Not even one. But I'll tell you this little fact. Bruno runs fast. Mostly on the beach, and always showing off. Oh, and here's another little fact. He brags. About everything. Including what a great *track star* he is. I'M A VERY ATHLETIC PERSON —*brag, brag.* Including what a great *dog trainer* he is. JUST HAND OVER YOUR DOG FOR A DAY. I GUARANTEE RESULTS —*brag, brag.* It gets on your nerves, all that showing off and bragging.

Once in a while, when I have nothing better to do, I run a little on the beach. Not that I could ever keep up with someone like Bruno. IF YOU WANT SOME GOOD COMPANY, I say, YOU'LL HAVE TO SLOW DOWN. Or at least I used to say that, when we were friends. Which we aren't anymore. Sometimes, before Bruno managed to ruin everything, we'd go all the way down to the army base at Camp Mitchel. They learn how to be good soldiers there, how to be brave. There's a really tall fence, and a big front gate and a whole bunch of guards guarding the gate, but if you hide behind the right sand dune, you can watch. You know what's embarrassing? When you cry in front of a boy. Which I did, unfortunately, in front of Bruno. I did it a bunch of times. It's the wounded ones, the soldiers they send back from the war. Some of them can't even *walk* anymore, or *see* anymore.

You try not to stare. But you wind up crying anyway.

Most of the time I look kind of regular: red shorts, checkered shirts, streaky blond ponytail, skinny feet. That's my regular self. But the day we found the baby, I was, well, a *prettier* version of me in my powder-blue dress for the party. Usually I don't go to a lot of parties, not the way some girls do, the popular ones. But this was different. This was a *library* party. The whole town was invited—even summer people—and no one's left out. I'd been waiting and waiting for August 31 and *finally* it was here. WE HAVE TO LEAVE, MARTHA. *NOW,* MARTHA. WE HAVE TO BE THE FIRST ONES THERE. OUR PICTURE MIGHT BE IN THE *BELLE BEACH PRESS!* That's what I told Martha. I had to tell her a bunch of times, but it worked. We were the first ones there.

Except, of course, for the baby.

I picked her up. And the minute I did —
the minute I picked up the baby — I forgot
about the library, the *Belle Beach Press,* and
everything else. She needed me. And I
needed to go someplace to think. That's
when I thought of the beach. And once
I was on the beach, I figured I'd just keep
going . . . all the way to Camp Mitchel.

Martha

ONE TIME ONLY, MARTHA. That's what they said. I could come with them *one time only*. Also they made me promise and swear. I PROMISE AND SWEAR NOT TO TELL ON YOU, JULIE. I PROMISE AND SWEAR NOT TO TELL ON YOU, BRUNO. Then we walked a million miles in the hot sand to a tall fence. Bruno read the big, scary sign: CAMP MITCHEL ARMY BASE AND HOSPITAL KEEP OUT BY ORDER OF THE U.S. ARMY. Then we were *spying*. We saw brave soldiers. And pretty nurses. I waved to the nurses, but Julie said, NO WAVING, MARTHA. SPIES DON'T WAVE.

Bruno

Ever since I was a little kid, I like running. I'm pretty fast. I was even kind of famous last spring — for a few hours, anyway — due to this thing I did in gym. Two hundred meters in 26.81 seconds. Which might have set some school record. Not that anyone thought to give me a trophy. My favorite place for running is the beach. Even in winter. My friend Kevin, he runs a lot, too. Lately, though, he's only interested in one thing. Which is *talking to girls.* Believe it or not, a lot of them talk back. Not that it matters to me. Let him talk to a *thousand* girls, I'll just run alone. When you run alone on the beach, alongside the big old Atlantic Ocean, you get happy for a while, even if you're not a great conversation starter like Kevin. When it's windy, I like that — the wind in my face. My legs are skinny but strong. Ben, my brother, he's twenty and strong everywhere, lots of muscles. He shaves every other day. I've watched him do it a million times, so if I ever get lucky and find some hairs on my face, I know what to do. Those posters you see around town, the ones that say things like I WANT YOU FOR THE U.S. ARMY, I love those. I'll definitely be enlisting in the U.S. Army. I might fly planes. I've always wanted to fly a plane. My parents won't like that, I guess. Two sons in the war, all those letters they have to write, and who knows *when* I have time to write back. But they'll be proud of me, too, the way they're proud of Ben. I'll be a big shot with the girls.

Girls. I'm no expert, if that's what you're thinking. I should be used to them by now but lately they have this weird effect on me, starting with my face burning up. Even if a girl says something ordinary such as HI, BRUNO, my face burns up, and if I say something back, it sounds completely idiotic. Or just the opposite happens and *nothing* comes out. It's like I can't even concentrate. Some girls, they get all personal. I hate that. Julie Sweet, she's like that, showing up on the beach, asking all these questions such as HEY, WHERE'RE YOU GOING, BRUNO? NOWHERE? FINE, I'LL COME, TOO. So then I'm walking on the beach —where everyone can see me —with Julie. She does 100 percent of the talking. About boring stuff, such as school (who talks about school in summer?), or some park in New York, or how she once got lost in the Museum of Natural History, as if I care. One time, she shows up on the beach with muffins. Normally, that would be a nice thing to do. But *her* muffins come with rules: THEY'RE BLUEBERRY, BRUNO, AND I MADE THEM MYSELF. HERE, *SMELL*, DON'T THEY SMELL GOOD! NOT NOW, BRUNO! WE CAN'T EAT THEM NOW. NOT YET, NOT UNTIL WE GET TO CAMP MITCHEL. So we finally get there, and I'm overly starving by this time, and she finally gives me one. It's really good. Not that I go out of my way to tell her that. We eat and watch the soldiers marching around, saluting. If you get hurt bad in the war, they send you to the hospital there for R & R. Rest and rehabilitation. Once, we saw a soldier with one arm. Once we saw a soldier, no legs. I thought about Ben's arms.

Ben's legs. Julie said, LET'S PRAY. And we did. Not out loud or anything. I guess you call that silent praying.

That was before she got mad at me. Before she stole the baby and took it to the beach. Before this old lady stepped out of the car that was parked on the beach.

5.

THE DOGS OF BELLE BEACH

Julie

George would never run away. Not in a million years; he's not that kind of dog. All his life, his whole entire life in the city, he never even *tried* it. Then we came to Belle Beach. We came for the summer, to this cottage on the beach, and on the very first day, George ran away.

It's because he didn't like it here. Whenever George doesn't like something, he pouts. Which is just like Martha. Whenever she doesn't like something, same thing. So as soon as we arrived, the very first *minute* practically, he got pouty and moody, and refused to eat. He also refused to take a walk on the beach *or* swim in the ocean. *Or* make friends with other dogs. It was frustrating but I gave him a nice little pep talk, the way Pop talks to me when I'm nervous sometimes, such as the night before the first day of school. I was gentle. DON'T WORRY, GEORGE. I was sweet. IT'S TRUE YOU'RE A CITY DOG, BUT YOU'LL GET USED TO IT HERE. George licked my salty fingers for a while.

Then he ran away.

Well, he didn't get too far. Just to the house next door. You could see him rolling around on the porch over there with his tongue hanging out, and some boy was there, too, rubbing George's ears. (The boy, it turns out, was Bruno. But I didn't know that until later.) I told George to come on home, he was disturbing the neighbors, but he completely ignored me as usual, and stayed where he was with his feet in the air. *Fine,* I thought. *Go live with* him *if you think he's so great. See if I care.*

That was the one and only time George ran away. Until that morning, the morning we found the baby. This time, he was mad. I bet he was *really* mad when we left for the library without him. And lonely. I bet he was *so* lonely. And that's why he ran away. So he could find us. And we all found each other on the beach! And you can't believe all the licking and kissing and making up! George even rolled over when I said ROLL OVER, GEORGE, which is the first time he ever did that! Then all of a sudden someone is climbing out of this *car* on the beach, and I guess I'm in shock or something, due to the shock of seeing her. It's possible I even stop breathing for a while. Yes, I definitely stop breathing when I see her.

Martha

My dog George eats sand, even when you say a thousand times in a row DON'T EAT SAND, GEORGE . . . and he's too scared to go in the ocean, even when you say a thousand times in a row TRY IT, YOU'LL LIKE IT, GEORGE! Once he ate a *library* book, chewed it *bad,* and we had to pay a fine at the library. But he would never eat a baby. And you know what? That morning on the beach, he sniffed our little baby — *sniff, sniff* — and wagged — *wag, wag* — and licked — *lick, lick* — her two big toes! The baby loved George. Everybody loves my George.

Bruno

We don't even have a dog. We used to. We used to have Doc, and Doc was totally great. But then he broke my father's heart — Doc did — and that's why the Ben-Eli family will never have another dog. Because of my father's broken heart.

Last year, my teacher Mrs. Miller made us write a short, interesting biography about someone in your family. It had to be three pages long. Can you believe that? *And* spelling counts, *and* punctuation. THIS IS SO STUPID AND SO UNFAIR AND STUPID. That's what I told my mother, who gave me her usual mom advice. I SUGGEST YOU SIT YOURSELF DOWN, BRUNO, AND *START WRITING.* She was in the middle of a letter to Ben. Every night after dinner, my mom writes to Ben. She writes at the kitchen table. Which is where I do my homework. So does Ben, when he's not in the war. I closed my eyes and tried to picture my brother, but you know who popped up instead? *Doc.* Next thing you know, I'm writing a short, interesting biography about Doc. Here's how it starts. DOC WENT TO WORK WITH MY DAD EVERY DAY AND THEY LEFT AT SIX IN THE MORNING. Exactly three pages later, here's how it ends. ONCE DOC'S RED BALL WAS LOST AT SEA. HE WAITED AND WATCHED THE SEA AND WAITED AND WATCHED, AND FINALLY, ONE HOUR LATER, IT WASHED UP ON THE BEACH. DOC HAD FAITH. Not bad, right? And nothing sad.

Not a word about the truck coming out of nowhere that day. Nobody cries, not in this biography — no broken hearts. It's 100 percent *happy*. Still, my mom got all mushy when she read it, and Dad. Mrs. Miller gave me a B+ instead of the A+ I deserved, due to SOME RATHER CAREFREE SPELLING, BRUNO, AND HANDWRITING ISSUES. Then she made me read it out loud at Friday Assembly. Which I didn't appreciate. BRUNO WRITES FROM THE HEART, she told the *entire* assembly. Which I also didn't appreciate. Afterward, I stuffed all three pages in a shoebox in my closet with Doc's red ball.

ALL DOGS SHOULD LIVE TO BE A THOUSAND. I said that to Julie one time. It's maybe the *only* time she agreed with anything I said. I said it during one of the training sessions I was giving George, free of charge. Training him was my idea.

George needed help getting used to the beach life. Free of charge — *not* my idea. Especially when you are doing the hard work of teaching him not to eat sand. I don't mind helping George, but let's face facts: money is money. Which I *tried* explaining to Julie. USUALLY I GET PAID FOR MY SERVICES — *hint, hint* — I GET PAID A LOT. But Julie didn't care about money. Especially *my* money. All she cared about was how soon I could get George to be a proper Belle Beach dog. Which just wasn't happening. Not until we got to Lesson #4, the title of which is "Heel, George." I gave him the usual pep talk. OKAY, PAL! HERE'S YOUR BIG CHANCE TO LEARN SOMETHING FROM A MASTER. Only this time when I said HEEL, GEORGE, he actually did it. Even Julie could see I was making him smart. She still didn't pay up, in case you were wondering about that.

Basically, George is a little on the lazy side, for a dog. But that morning, the morning everything happened, I discovered this whole *other* side of George. He looked real *serious* when I spotted him coming down the beach—that's the first thing that got my attention. Because George never looks serious. He wasn't racing down the beach or anything like that, but it's true he was moving a whole lot faster than usual, as if he had something important to do. Which also got my attention since George never has something important to do. Anyway, George didn't see me. Not yet. He was too busy checking out this big black car on the beach. I was also checking it out, from my own little vantage point behind a dune, and by the way, there's a law about cars on the beach. *NO* CARS ON THE BEACH, that's a Belle Beach law. Someone was breaking it, and the question is *who*. Who's in that car? Maybe some *spy,* some enemy spy. Well, I'm about to find out because someone (he might be an actual *chauffeur,* the kind you see in the movies) is opening the back door of the car. An old lady gets out. She gets out slowly, feetfirst, and when all of her is out, I'm thinking *not your typical spy.* I take note of her clunky brown shoes and long blue dress. In case I need that information for later. I also take note of the fact that she's really tall. Most of the old ladies you see around town are pretty short.

Company. All of a sudden the spy's got *company.* More specifically, it's Julie, Martha, the baby, and George. I'm too far away to hear what they're saying, but I know there's a whole lot of talking going on. Meanwhile, the *chauffeur* — or whatever he is — is unfolding this blanket next to the car. He puts down this big picnic basket. Shoes come off, and next thing you know, everyone's sitting on the blanket. Even George. Even the tall lady. Speaking of which, I'm beginning to get this weird feeling: *Hey, don't I know that old lady? I'm pretty sure I've seen her before!* The real question is *where. Where* have I seen her before? Then a whole bunch of things happen really fast. Beginning with me *sneezing,* and it's a pretty loud sneeze. George looks up and starts barking hello. Julie looks up and gives me this ferocious *I know you've been following me* face. Martha whispers something to the lady, who immediately starts waving the kind of wave that means, *Come on over here, young man . . . seems to me we have something to talk about.* Well, I don't have much of a choice, do I? So I go on over there.

6.

SUMMER
PEOPLE

Julie

We took the train to Belle Beach. Pop, me, Martha, plus George. We took the 11:05 from Pennsylvania Station, and there were so many soldiers on the train. They all loved George! HEY, BUDDY, YOU REMIND ME OF MY DOG BACK HOME — that kind of thing. The soldiers played cards and blew smoke out the open windows. They talked to Pop about how they would soon be SHIPPED OVERSEAS ANY DAY NOW and were MISS- ING THAT GIRL OF MINE ALREADY, AND MY GRANDMA'S APPLE PIE. Pop took pic- tures as usual, and wrote in his little brown book as usual. The conductor was a lady. NEXT STOP, BELLE BEACH! BELLE BEACH, NEXT STOP! We got off the train and waved to the soldiers going to war. They all waved back and so did the lady conductor and then we were here.

Coming here, Pop's idea. THERE'S THIS LITTLE TOWN ON LONG ISLAND, he said. SUN, SAND, AND A QUIET PLACE FOR ME TO FINISH MY BOOK. Some people such as movie stars are extremely famous. My pop is a little famous. It's because his name is on three different books. All three are in the New York Public Library! Plus, you see his name sometimes in a *magazine* such as *Life* magazine.

I like the title of his book that will be number four: *Every One a Hero*. That's a really good title. It's about the war and brave soldiers and serious things. Pop says writing a book is *hard work*. Way harder than school, and you can hear him up there, typing away on the upstairs deck. All day and sometimes at night, it's *click, click, click . . . click, click, click.* And I take care of Martha.

I'm not a great artist or anything, but I like to draw. I have this sketch pad. Red cover, and I bought it with my own money and it's just for Belle Beach. If you walk around with a sketch pad, you look important and people want to be your friend. And before you know it, you've got a lot of new friends! Well, that's what I *thought* would happen. But it's hard to make a friend in a place like Belle Beach. Everybody knows everybody else, and you're just one of the summer people, so no one talks to you. Oh well, who cares? I have plenty of friends in New York. Hundreds! Those four girls on that old green blanket on the beach every day? Why would I be friends with them? George walked down to their blanket one time. LOOK AT HIS LONG FLOPPY EARS, they laughed. LOOK AT HIS FUNNY FAT FEET! I hate those girls. So does George.

Martha

I go there every day. To the big house next door. And George comes, too. Mrs. Ben-Eli is my friend. COME ON IN, MARTHA, DOOR'S OPEN. That's what she says when I am peeking in the door with George. They have lemonade over there, and Mrs. Ben-Eli likes books. I like books, too. I like them a lot, so she reads to me and I read to her and she always says, YOU'RE A TERRIFIC READER, MARTHA. I'm allowed to cut out pictures from her old magazines. One time I found a picture of Eleanor Roosevelt eating *pink clouds on angel food cake*. I cut it out for Julie. I cut out the recipe, too. And gave it to Julie and said, LET'S BAKE A CAKE! But Julie said, NOT NOW, MARTHA. It's her favorite thing to say: NOT NOW, MARTHA. Sometimes I look for seashells on the beach with Mrs. Ben-Eli. If she holds my hand, I like that. One time there was a letter in her pocket from Ben. IF YOU WANT, YOU COULD READ ME BEN'S LETTER, I said. So we sat in the sand and she read it to me. When it was over, I said, DON'T CRY, MRS. BEN-ELI. HE'LL COME HOME SOON.

Bruno

Ben-Eli, that's my last name. It's also the name of our family business. Which is Ben-Eli's Grand Market, but most people just call it Ben-Eli's. It's across the street from the post office. You can't miss it. There's a big green awning out front: BEN-ELI'S GRAND MARKET. All year long my parents look forward to *the season*. Meaning summertime, when Belle Beach is *bursting at the seams with summer people,* and they all need things, a lot of which they buy at Ben-Eli's. Mostly they buy food. But other stuff, too — from the Necessary Summer Sundries aisle — pails and shovels, beach towels, sunglasses.

Working at Ben-Eli's this summer — making sandwiches for the lunch crowd — *my* idea. It's an important job. It used to be Ben's job, three summers in a row, before the war, and he used to let me help sometimes, like putting mustard on bread. I'm pretty good with the mustard. 11:30 to 1:30, that's my shift. Customers line up and I get to say things like I'LL BE WITH YOU IN A MOMENT, MA'AM. Or, YES, SIR! ONE CHEESE SANDWICH COMING RIGHT UP! Some days I make thirty sandwiches in a row. I wrap them in brown paper, to go. A lot of kids would want money for all that work. Not me. The day he hired me, I told my father, YOU DON'T HAVE TO PAY ME. NOT UNLESS YOU WANT TO. I said, THIS IS A *FAMILY* BUSINESS. I'M DOING IT FOR

THE *FAMILY*. I waited around to see what he had to say about my generosity. I waited a long time and finally he said, YOU ARE A GOOD WORKER AND ENTITLED TO A SALARY, BRUNO. The amount wasn't too much.

It was June 21. I know it was June 21 because it was the first day of summer vacation, and also my first day on the job, and I was feeling pretty good about both of those things. After my shift, I walked over to Front Street, to the train station. I like to see who's getting on or off the trains. Sometimes it's people you know. Other times — especially the first days of summer — it's people you don't know. You could say I have a curious streak. Which is a good thing to have if you're going to be a newspaper reporter. Which I might decide to be. Plus a veterinarian, so I can take care of sick dogs. But that's not the point. The point is, a ton of people got off the 1:45 from the city that day. Summer people mostly, strangers in hot city clothes. They come with their big suitcases and move into the cottages up and down the beach. Once in a while you spot a possible friend, some no-name city kid, but mostly you don't. Not that it matters. Because they all leave anyway, as soon as summer's over.

First, I noticed the dog. The long droopy ears, short stubby legs, big feet. Basset hound maybe, and he was getting off the train—the 1:45—with these two summer girls. Later on, I'm out on my porch and there they are again, all three of them, at the cottage next door. *Just my luck*, I thought, *girls next door.* I'm trying to figure out how to get the dog to come over—dog only, no girls—and that's when I see Tess. Ben's

Tess, walking on the beach. *Are you back? Is it you? Did you finally come back?* I open my mouth but nothing comes out. It's windy on the beach and Tess keeps walking, into the wind, farther and farther away.

7.

BINOCULARS

Julie

I don't even like boys that much. Especially unfriendly boys. Which is the definition of Bruno. Or at least it *was* the definition of Bruno when we first came to Belle Beach. Not that I cared about some kid next door. Why would I?

Then one day I found this rusty old bike on the beach. Nobody wanted it. You could tell no one cared. So I dragged it home and cleaned it up. It took a long time and a lot of soap and water, and when I was finally done cleaning it up, it still looked rusty. It still looked old. But at least I had a bike and

I could ride it to town and try a few things I don't normally try in the city. Such as taking my hands off the handlebars. And pedaling crazy fast. And ringing the bell a thousand times loud. I liked being alone for a change. No Martha. No George. It was a really good time. Until the bike decides to go all *wobbly* on me, and next thing you know, I'm flying. Not too much blood, just the usual knee and elbow stuff. Turns out someone saw the whole thing. Like an actual witness. The someone was Bruno. Yes, that Bruno, the unfriendly neighbor boy. Which would normally be completely humiliating. Only it wasn't. Because Bruno didn't laugh at me the way a lot of boys would. He just picked up the bike. Stood there saying nothing for a while. And left.

So that's when we started being friends. When Bruno didn't laugh at me.

Later that day I saw him again, from

our upstairs deck. He was out on the beach, facing the ocean, and these big binoculars were kind of *plastered* to his eyes. At first I thought it was some soldier out there, not Bruno. My knees hurt, due to my little flying event, and also my right elbow, but I ran down to the beach. I *had* to try those binoculars.

Martha

Binoculars have *magical powers!* You have to take them everywhere. All around Belle Beach. And then one day you'll *see* her! And she'll be perfect! And you'll say, WILL YOU BE MY MOTHER and she'll say, YES, MARTHA, I WILL BE YOUR NEW MOTHER. Julie doesn't care about binoculars too much. She says, OUR FAMILY IS FINE JUST THE WAY IT IS, MARTHA. Julie is wrong. We need one more.

Bruno

The first time Martha came over, she came alone. No sister. No dog. Just Martha. I knew her name by then, but I had no idea what she was doing on my porch at six in the morning. I wasn't exactly thrilled to see her there, since I was in the middle of doing something important. That being push-ups, which, for the record, I do twenty of every day. Martha circled the porch a few times, humming. You had the feeling something was going to happen, and after a few more circles and a few more push-ups, it did. It wasn't a huge thing that happened—she put her face flat against the screen door and wanted to know if she could see the *mother of the house* —but you couldn't exactly ignore it. MOM! I called. HEY, MOM, YOU HAVE A VISITOR! My mother opened the door, took one look at Martha, and smiled. MORNING, MARTHA. She was holding a jar of jam. WOULD YOU LIKE TO COME IN? I WAS JUST MAKING TOAST.

After that, Martha came over a lot. In the morning before my mom goes to work at the library, Martha. I MADE THIS PICTURE FOR YOU, MRS. BEN-ELI! Dinnertime, when my mom is cooking dinner, Martha. I FOUND THIS FLOWER FOR YOU, MRS. BEN-ELI! One time, I caught her on the beach with Ben's binoculars. THOSE ARE BEN'S, I said. Martha didn't flinch. *Or* lower the binoculars. MRS. BEN-ELI LETS ME USE THEM, she said. WHENEVER I WANT.

So my own mother was practically giving away Ben's binoculars.

Wide-awake. That's me these days. Wide-awake, at five in the morning. Which isn't as bad as it sounds, because my parents are still asleep and I have the whole house to myself. Ben's room is the one next to mine, and I have to go in there to make sure everything is just the way he left it, for when he comes home. Eight baseball banners on wall over his bed: *check*. Seven high school trophies in bookcase: *check*. Five college books on desk: *check*. Two secret letters from Tess in bottom dresser drawer: *check*. Some mornings I grab Ben's binoculars and go out to the half-dark beach and look around. If you keep looking for a long time, you can almost see Ben coming up the beach, swinging his duffel and waving. You can almost see Ben, home from the war.

YOU HAVE TO GIVE THEM BACK, that's what I told Martha. YOU HAVE TO GIVE THEM BACK WHEN BEN COMES HOME. I told her five or six times, so she wouldn't forget.

8.

MARTHA, QUEEN OF ICE CREAM

Julie

One morning Martha woke up with a sore throat. It was so sore she wouldn't eat breakfast even though it was pancakes. So sore she wouldn't put on her favorite pink bathing suit, the one she wears *every* day, even when it's raining all day. Normally, Pop is typing away on his book and taking pictures every day. But on the day of Martha's sore throat, he sat on the white wicker couch instead, holding Martha. RUN NEXT DOOR, JULIE. THE BEN-ELIS WILL KNOW A GOOD LOCAL DOCTOR, he said.

I ran next door. Bruno was doing his usual: calisthenics on the porch. Including jumping jacks. MARTHA'S SICK, I said. MOM, he called through the screen door. HEY, MOM!—*jump, jump*—MARTHA'S SICK!

Dr. Chase was old. Just like our doctor in New York, Dr. Mason. He had the same black bag and said MMHMMM like Dr. Mason when he looked in Martha's throat. After looking around for a while, the news was bad. *Tonsils.* Martha's tonsils had to come out. Martha cried and clung to Pop. Then Dr. Chase said the magic word. *Ice cream.* AFTERWARD WE SERVE *ICE CREAM,* he told Martha. AS MUCH AS YOU CAN EAT.

So Martha and Pop went for an overnight at the Good Samaritan Hospital, and George and I went for an overnight at the Ben-Elis'. It was my first overnight ever, so I had to give myself a little pep talk, along

the lines of: *Julie, you may not be homesick.*
You are much too old to be homesick. Which
definitely worked. I was my usual cheerful
self, plus an excellent guest. I set the table
for dinner, even though nobody asked me
to, and scraped carrots, even though I'm
terrible at scraping carrots. Mrs. Ben-Eli
cooked hamburgers, which I like, and pota-
toes, which I like, and carrots. But when
dinner was finally on the table that I set, I
wasn't that hungry. Bruno sat there stuff-
ing food in his mouth, saying absolutely
nothing the whole time. Not that it made
the slightest difference to me. At seven we
all huddled around the radio, even George,
and President Roosevelt talked about the
war. I like his deep voice and I like when he
says things about *standing united and strong.*
Mr. Ben-Eli made a circle in the middle of
the big world map tacked to the kitchen
wall. IF MY CALCULATIONS ARE RIGHT,

BEN'S BATTALION SHOULD BE RIGHT ABOUT *HERE,* he said, tapping the circle, and then he said, GOD BLESS. Mrs. Ben-Eli closed her eyes and whispered it, too, GOD BLESS.

The guest room was yellow and the moon was a half-moon that night. I pulled George onto the bed. Which he liked. And hugged him close. Which he liked. But all of a sudden he got up and left, to sleep down the hall with Bruno. *Who cares about you?* I thought, and started to cry. Which was totally babyish, of course. I wanted Pop. And cried some more, pushing my face in the pillow so no one would hear, especially Bruno. Then I heard Mrs. Ben-Eli at the door. JULIE?—*knock, knock*—I'VE BROUGHT A LITTLE SOMETHING, TO HELP YOU SLEEP. It was ice cream—two dips—in a green bowl. And *I* wasn't even the one with tonsillitis.

When Martha came home without her tonsils, she was allowed to have ice cream whenever she wanted, even first thing in the morning. So we were always running out and I was always riding my bike into town for more. The little pink ice-cream shop — Snowflake — is next to the train station. Sometimes Bruno was there with that friend of his, Kevin, and he completely ignored me. Of course I completely ignored him back. Bruno wasn't there, though, the first time I saw Tess. Only I didn't know her name yet, or who she was, or what was in her basket. She was coming out of Snowflake that day in July and all I could think was *she's so beautiful . . . why can't I be beautiful, too?* Then the train came clanking into the station — the 3:35 to New York — and she was running for the train. *Come back!* I thought. *We'll be friends!* But she stepped on board. And never even knew when something blew out of her basket.

By the time I picked it up (It was a little white hat. For a doll maybe? Or a baby?) the 3:35 was moving down the track. I put it in my pocket. In case she came back.

Martha

When you go to the hospital, they give you ice cream! And Pop makes you a crown that says MARTHA, QUEEN OF ICE CREAM! And Julie gives you a picture of the beach that she drew! And the Ben-Elis come over for a party! And George isn't sad anymore. Because now you are home.

Bruno

Some people are good at everything. They pitch like a major league pitcher and catch like a major league catcher and hit home runs and get straight As and shave. My brother is that kind of person. Then last summer, a whole year ago when I'm only eleven, I'm making myself a sandwich at Ben-Eli's. It's afternoon and the lunch crowd is gone and Ben is sweeping up. It's a pretty big store, and when the front door opens, this little bell rings and wherever you are, you hear *ding, ding!* So it rings for the thousandth time that day — *ding,*

ding!—and in walks this girl eating an enormous ice-cream cone. Strawberry triple-scoop. She's older than me, more like Ben. Speaking of Ben, he's pretending not to look, but he's looking, all right. Next thing you know, the broom disappears and he's talking to the girl, making her laugh. It's a pretty nice laugh. I take a few bites of my sandwich. They talk some more, and there's that laugh again. I pour some milk and mind my own business. Still, you can't help hearing things. Like her name, which is Tess, and it's a pretty nice name. You hear other things, too. Such as this: I JUST GOT OFF THE TRAIN FROM NEW YORK. And this: I'M ON MY WAY TO CAMP MITCHEL, TO STUDY AT THE NURSING SCHOOL THERE. And Ben's big offer, you hear that, too. I'D BE HAPPY TO DRIVE YOU. IT'S JUST UP THE ROAD. MY CAR'S OUT FRONT. . . .

Ben. That's my brother. He gets As and home runs and trophies. And the keys to my father's car . . . so he can drive a girl named Tess to nursing school.

9.

THE JEEP AND THE YELLOW CONVERTIBLE

Julie

Her name is Miss Bancroft, but we call her
The Driver and she's always on time. Ten
o'clock sharp. She comes three days a week
and her car is a big army jeep. She drives
Pop to Camp Mitchel, past the guards,
so he can interview the soldiers there.
EVERY SINGLE SOLDIER HAS A STORY,
Pop says. Of course Martha turns into
this sad little sad sack when he leaves. So
I take her next door. Grown-ups always
love Martha. Especially Mrs. Ben-Eli. You
can tell, the minute she opens the door. I
WAS JUST THINKING ABOUT YOU TWO,

HOPING YOU'D STOP BY, that kind of thing. We just kind of follow her around for a while. One time she was knitting a scarf for Ben. HE'LL NEED TO BE WARM OVER THERE, COME WINTER, she said. Another time, she was making red checks on a long list of books she was ordering for the new children's library. IT'S A LABOR OF LOVE, she said, MY WORK AT THE LIBRARY. Then there was the time we watched her write a letter — an actual *letter* — to Eleanor Roosevelt! She wrote, I AM THE MOTHER OF A BRAVE YOUNG MAN STATIONED OVERSEAS. I WANT TO PERSONALLY THANK YOU FOR YOUR SELF-LESS TRIPS TO VISIT OUR TROOPS IN THE PACIFIC. YOU BOOST THEIR SPIRITS, AND MINE. Mrs. Ben-Eli folded up the letter to mail and said, HOW NICE IT WOULD BE TO MEET HER SOMEDAY. I never knew she would want to meet Eleanor Roosevelt.

When Mrs. Ben-Eli goes off to work at the library, Martha and I go down to the ocean with pails and shovels, the beach ball, and George. Mostly, though, we're just waiting for noon, when Pop comes back. Martha keeps looking at my watch. WHEN WILL IT BE NOON, JULIE, WHEN WILL IT BE NOON? And finally it is. HERE'S YOUR POP, says The Driver. SAFE AND SOUND! One time they were late. Really, really late and I was really, really mad. DON'T BLAME ME, joked Pop. WE GOT A FLAT — *joke, joke* — AND WE HAD TO CHANGE OUR FLAT TIRE! *We* got a flat. *Our* flat tire.

Martha

Miss Bancroft is in the army, I think, and her lipstick is called Red Roses! One time she let Julie and me sit in the jeep! First we sat in the back seat. Then we sat in the front seat. Then we sat in back again. I'M NEVER GETTING OUT, I said. Miss Bancroft turned on the radio and there was singing on the radio! Then Pop got in the front seat, and they went away and Julie took me to the beach. We made a thousand sandcastles.

When it rains in Belle Beach, I get to go

to the movies with Julie. One time there was *kissing in the movies!* POP SHOULD KISS MISS BANCROFT, I said. DON'T BE RIDICULOUS, Julie said. POP IS NOT A MOVIE.

Bruno

If my dad ever finds out, no big deal. But if my mom finds out, I'm *cooked*. It happened last year when I was eleven, and it was after Ben enlisted but before he went overseas. Okay, that day he's driving me home from Kevin's and it's just the two of us in my father's old yellow convertible and the top is down so the wind is blowing Ben's words around, but a few words stick. Words like NEW YORK... GOING TO THE CITY TONIGHT... I HAVE TO SEE TESS BEFORE I'M SHIPPED OUT.... Then all of a sudden he pulls into this empty parking lot behind Belle Beach High School and says, WANNA DRIVE, BRUNO? Are you *kidding* me! Then Ben gives me an *actual driving lesson*! Me! Driving! Forward. Stop. Right turn. Forward. Stop. Left turn. Forward. Stop. I never wanted it to end. I was pretty good, by the way, Ben said I was good. His exact words: NOT BAD, BRUNO. NOT BAD AT ALL, FOR A BRAND-NEW DRIVER. It was the greatest day of my life. My dad is the kind of person who would appreciate a good story like that, so maybe I'll tell him someday. If my mom finds out, I'm *cooked*.

10.

STARRY NIGHTS

Julie

I love our little cottage, especially the upstairs deck. You can see the world up there. The sand and the sea and moon and the stars at night and maybe even Jupiter. One night, I decide to do something exciting for a change. I'M MAKING MYSELF A SLEEP-OUT ON THE UPSTAIRS DECK, I say. JUST ME AND THE STARS. Pop and Martha watch me pack and they both make a point of looking a little too sad, too left out. I'M JUST GOING UPSTAIRS, NOT TO *AUSTRALIA*, I say and start up the stairs.

That's when Martha starts with the *sobbing*. Which, of course, is a lot louder, a lot more *tragic,* than her regular crying. I'LL MISS YOU SO MUCH, JULIE —*sob, sob*— I WANT TO SLEEP UNDER THE STARS, TOO —*sob, sob*. Honestly, the sound of Martha sobbing like that, it makes you feel terrible. It makes you feel mean, and I hate feeling mean, so I back down the stairs, put an arm around Martha, and say: OKAY, FINE, EVERY-ONE'S INVITED. INCLUDING GEORGE. More packing: blankets and pillows and the big flashlight and cookies and hot cocoa in a thermos, because even though it's summer, we all like cocoa. Stubborn old George refuses to climb the stairs, so we sing his good-night song —*GOOD NIGHT, SWEET GEORGE! GOOD NIGHT, SWEET GEORGE!*—and leave him in the kitchen. But about two minutes later, he comes on up, curls into Martha, and goes snoring off to sleep. Then Pop clicks on the flashlight and tells the scariest ghost story you ever want to hear, and Martha and I are *squeezing* each other and shaking! When the story is over, Pop falls asleep — *snore, snore.* Then Martha — *snore, snore.* So now everyone's sleeping but me. I stare at the sky, looking for stars, but there *are* none that night. No stars. No one to talk to. Nothing to do. I'm just thinking what an idiotic idea this was after all, that *nothing* exciting ever happens to me, when something finally happens. Rain! Pouring, soaking rain! Now everyone's up! Everyone's drenched! And yelling and running downstairs, even George!

And that, my friends, is the end of the Sweet Family Sleep-Out.

I like the sound of the ocean at night. You can see the whole beach, right to the end of Long Island, if the moon is out bright. Like the night I saw Pop and Miss Bancroft out there, sitting on our big beach blanket.

Martha

One night I couldn't fall asleep. And I still couldn't fall asleep. And I *still* couldn't fall asleep. So Pop took me for a walk on the beach at *midnight!* We saw five million stars! Then Pop told me a secret! This is the secret: ONE SUMMER, A LONG TIME AGO, I WAS WALKING ON THE BEACH—THIS VERY SAME BEACH—AND IT WAS DEFINITELY MY LUCKY DAY, BECAUSE IT'S HERE I MET YOUR MOTHER. HERE ON THE BEACH. HER BATHING SUIT WAS RED. Then we went home and I got in my bed. Then I got out again. And snuggled up close to Julie in her bed and tickled her ear. WAKE UP, JULIE! I KNOW A GOOD SECRET ABOUT MOMMY! WAKE UP NOW! But she wouldn't wake up.

Bruno

Ben and Tess. Tess and Ben. On the beach, holding hands. You see them from your bedroom window, and when you're standing on the porch. Summer was nearly over, and when it was, Tess would be going home to New York, to the boardinghouse on East 39th Street. A house for *independent young ladies,* she called it. They were always holding hands. Even in line at the movie theater. Even inside Snowflake. Even in front of my parents, at the kitchen table, when Tess came to dinner those times. And always on the beach. It wasn't like I went out of my *way* to follow them. Why would I? But there they were — the night she graduated nursing school — side by side in the sand. I see her white cap in the sand, thanks to the moon and all the bright stars that night.

11.

KEVIN'S THREE BROTHERS

Julie

THREE OF THEM ARE ENLISTED MEN.
Bruno told me that. About Kevin's brothers. Kevin is his best friend. Not that Bruno
ever says it. Boys don't care about having
a best friend. Not the way girls do. I used
to have a best friend. Linda. We both have
April birthdays *and* green eyes *and* little
sisters. Then last year Linda pulled me
aside at recess and whispered, PRESIDENT
ROOSEVELT CALLED MY FATHER. WE
ARE MOVING AWAY SO MY FATHER CAN
DO SPECIAL SECRET *WAR WORK*, FOR
PRESIDENT ROOSEVELT. So Linda moved

away and that's why I don't have a best friend anymore.

Bruno's best friend, Kevin, is not my type. Talks too much. Oh, and if you want to hear a dumb joke, just ask Kevin. His mom's name is Charlotte but everyone calls her Charlie, which I know because I see her sometimes at the library. She's one of the Good Ladies. Which is short for the Good Ladies of Belle Beach Library Committee. There are *fourteen* of them, Kevin told me that. Fourteen Good Ladies building a new children's library. They paint and hammer and saw and drill. They even do plumbing, and they all report to Mrs. Ben-Eli. She's the boss of the library. Which Kevin told me but I already knew, and I even went to her *office*. I went to her office the day she made me a Junior Library Volunteer. If you want to be one, if Mrs. Ben-Eli picks you, you have to come to the library Tuesday and Saturday mornings from nine to noon. You wear a badge that says I AM A JUNIOR LIBRARY VOLUNTEER. Kevin's working, too, only his mother *makes* him volunteer and he won't wear his badge. One Saturday he told me *three* dumb jokes in a row. I pretended they were funny, all three.

Then something terrible happened. The worst thing in the world happened. One of Kevin's brothers died in the war.

The memorial was on the beach. They had it at sunrise and the whole town was there. Every single person, I think, even summer people. Pop woke us early that day so we could *pay our respects to the family*. The sky was pink and you couldn't see Kevin anywhere. Not until he stood on a bench to talk about his brother. You could hear people crying and sniffling, blowing noses. Dogs ran in and out of the ocean, barking. American flags, everywhere you looked, American flags. They were beautiful. There was a bugle.

Afterward, Pop took my hand and we walked up the beach for a while and Martha ran ahead. She did cartwheels in the sand. IT'S A GOOD THING YOU'RE OLD, I told Pop. YOU CAN'T BE AN ENLISTED MAN IF YOU'RE OLD. YOU CAN'T GO DYING IN THE WAR. When we got back to the cottage, I washed my hair, then Martha's. She yelled, as usual, when I combed out the tangles. And I told her, as usual, she better hold still. We dried our hair in the sun. Martha read out loud, something about President Roosevelt's dog. THE DOG'S NAME IS FALA, she read. Six years old and reading out loud for the last two years. Martha might be some kind of *genius.*

Martha

Pop and Julie were *serious,* so I was serious, too. A lot of people were crying. Even grown-ups. I hate when grown-ups cry.

Bruno

There's nothing we look forward to more than mail. That is a direct quote. And you know who wrote that in a letter to Kevin? His brother Paul. He wrote it before he died over there. *There's nothing we look forward to more than mail . . . so keep up the good work . . . keep sending those wonderful letters about everything that reminds me of home.*

Six. I've been to six of them altogether. Six memorials on the beach. All because of the war. I guess you could call it the Belle Beach way of saying goodbye to a hero. The first five were bad. But this was really bad.

This was *Paul's* memorial service, *Paul's* goodbye. *Paul,* the brother who taught Kevin how to ride a bike *and* float in the ocean the summer we were four. I didn't want to go. My parents kept saying things like KEVIN'S YOUR BEST FRIEND, BRUNO. WE SHOW UP FOR FRIENDS. I still didn't want to go and even faked a stomachache, faked throwing up. IT'S GOING TO BE A ROUGH DAY, they said. GO GET DRESSED. A million people showed up on the beach that day. It was hot and I was stuck in long pants and a jacket and tie, even though Paul's not the kind of guy who cares if you don't wear a tie. The priest from their church said a bunch of things about Paul. Most of which I couldn't hear because of the ocean and the waves and some little kids screaming somewhere. After the priest, Kevin got to talk. He talked loud, like he was shouting, and he read that letter from Paul, and I started to cry. Just so you know, I wasn't the only one crying. I couldn't stop and then my parents were *hugging* me. In public, can you believe they would actually do that? A lot of us went back to Kevin's house after. There was a ton of food. I was really starving and Kevin was, too, so we loaded up our plates a few times and it was really good food. Then we took off our ties and threw a ball around Kevin's yard until some girls from school came by and he decided to have, well, you know, a *conversation* with the girls. I went home. And walked around Ben's room for a while. I sat on his bed.

12.

ELEANOR
AND
ELEANOR

Julie

It was early in the morning and Mrs. Ben-Eli was walking all by herself on the beach. She looked lonely and I didn't want her to be lonely, so I caught up to her and said HI, MRS. BEN-ELI and she said HI, JULIE! The sky was pink. I LOVE THE BEACH AT SUNRISE, she said. ME, TOO, I said, I LOVE IT, TOO. Her sweater was red with a hood and mine was blue with a hood and the water rolled over our toes. I'M HOPING FOR A LETTER FROM BEN TODAY, said Mrs. Ben-Eli. IF YOU WANT, I COULD DO A LITTLE PRAYING, I said. I'LL PRAY YOU

GET A LETTER FROM BEN. Baby birds ran across the beach, making teeny little footprints in the sand. Mrs. Ben-Eli smiled at the baby birds and the teeny little footprints. Her hair was wavy and brown, just like my mother's. Usually I don't say too much about my mother, but that morning I told Mrs. Ben-Eli, MY MOTHER'S NAME WAS ELEANOR. JUST LIKE ELEANOR ROOSEVELT. Mrs. Ben-Eli smiled some more. WHAT A SPLENDID NAME, she said.

Martha

Pop took a picture of George on the beach. I'm in the picture, too! Doing a cartwheel in the sand! It's the best picture you ever want to see. I look at it fifty times every day! At night it goes under my pillow. I showed it to Mrs. Ben-Eli and Mr. Ben-Eli and Bruno, and they all like the picture of George on the beach and my cartwheel. I might send it to President Roosevelt. He doesn't like the war (Pop told me that), so my picture will make him happy. President Roosevelt likes dogs. And children. Mrs. Roosevelt likes them, too. Pop told me that. My pop knows *everything*.

Bruno

Leave it to my mom to put me to work at the library. THE GRAND OPENING IS JUST AROUND THE CORNER, BRUNO. A COUPLE OF HOURS A DAY, IT WON'T KILL YOU, she says. YOU'VE GOT PLENTY OF TIME ON YOUR HANDS. WE *NEED* YOU, she says.

My jobs over there are not exactly thrilling. I get to mop, then dust, then scrub, then mop some more. I get to lug books — millions of little kid books — and put them on shelves *in alphabetical order,* since the world might come to an end if they're not *in alphabetical order.* Sometimes Julie shows up. WANT SOME HELP,

BRUNO? I don't want help. Not that it stops her from trying to boss me around. WE HAVE TO PUT ALL THE HORSE BOOKS *HERE,* BRUNO. LINE THEM UP, NICE AND STRAIGHT, AND THE BOOKS ABOUT ABRAHAM LINCOLN GO *HERE,* WITH BIOGRAPHIES ABOUT FAMOUS PEOPLE. I make a point of doing the opposite of everything she says. It really annoys her. My mom is in charge of the library; she's the boss, and the Good Ladies have all these secret meetings in her office. The Good Ladies, that's short for the Good Ladies of Belle Beach Library Committee, and those meetings are about library stuff. You can't believe the fighting in there. They fight about everything, including the color of the new library cards, where to put the dictionary stand, and rules about pets in the library. One thing they don't fight about is who cuts the ribbon at the ribbon-cutting ceremony on August 31. They all say, MRS. BEN-ELI CUTS THE RIBBON. When they say it, I feel kind of proud of my mother.

So we're walking home after working hard at the library and Julie is talking about Eleanor Roosevelt again. Only she keeps calling her *Eleanor*, like they're personal friends or something. Julie: EVERY DAY, ELEANOR DOES SOMETHING *NICE*. SHE'S A VERY NICE PERSON. DID YOU KNOW THAT, BRUNO? Julie: ELEANOR VISITS AMERICAN SERVICEMEN OVERSEAS. EVEN THOUGH THERE ARE *BOMBS* OVERSEAS, AND SHE GOES TO *HOSPITALS* TO CHEER UP SICK SOLDIERS. And here comes the showstopper. WE'LL INVITE HER TO THE GRAND OPENING. IT WILL BE A BIG SURPRISE. FOR YOUR *MOTHER*, BRUNO.

I tell her I'm pretty sure *Eleanor* has

better things to do. But you know Julie, she never lets you talk. And that afternoon we're back in town again, at the post office mailing an actual *invitation* to Mrs. Roosevelt. The invitation, by the way, is made mostly by Julie, including a picture that she drew of the library. It's a pretty good picture. SHE'LL COME, Julie says. COUNT ON IT. She says it about a hundred more times on the long walk home.

A few weeks after that, and three days before the Grand Opening, I'm at the post office mailing something again. This time it's an actual *letter*, from me to Mrs. Roosevelt. And no, in case you're wondering, I don't tell Julie. Why would I? She isn't even *talking* to me by this time. Besides which, it's none of her business. I don't even know why I write it, to tell you the truth. I just *do*.

It's mostly about Ben. Stuff like *my*

brother's an enlisted man. I don't say my parents are way more worried than the usual amount due to no letters from Ben — not one — in five weeks and four days. I put a picture of Ben in the envelope with the letter. It's an old one — he's around ten, I guess, but it still looks like Ben. *If you see this kid next time you're visiting the troops, tell him hi from Bruno.* Before I seal the envelope, I add a little more: *Remember that invitation about the library? You never answered but you're still invited. August 31, remember? The whole town will be happy if you come. Especially my mom. That's her birthday by the way, August 31. Best birthday present would be Ben coming home. Second best, meeting Eleanor Roosevelt. The Good Ladies might even put your name on the library. They'll call it THE ELEANOR ROOSEVELT CHILDREN'S LIBRARY.* (This part I completely make up, but I figure it's worth a shot.) I signed it: *Your friend, Bruno*

Ben-Eli. Even though I'm not exactly *friends* with Eleanor Roosevelt.

I leave the letter at the post office, cross the street to Ben-Eli's, make a couple of sandwiches for my dad and me to eat in the stockroom. We eat and talk about baseball and hot-fudge sundaes, and how summer's nearly over, and Ben. I CAN'T WAIT TO PICK HIM UP AT THE TRAIN STATION, I say, THE DAY HE COMES HOME. My dad sucks in his breath and says, WHAT A DAY THAT WILL BE. Then the little bell rings — *ding, ding* — and he hurries to the front of the store, calling out, HELLO, MRS. HERMAN! HOW CAN WE HELP YOU TODAY?

13.

EXCELLENT
PEN PALS
AND OTHER
DISASTERS

Julie

The problem with pen pals? They don't write back. And I'll tell you this little fact: if someone goes to the trouble of writing you a letter, you're supposed to write back. It's called *manners*. Last spring everyone in my class got a soldier pen pal, and I am an excellent pen pal. SEND WARM GREETINGS FROM THE HOME FRONT AND YOU'RE DOING YOUR PART FOR THE WAR EFFORT! That's what they told us and that's what I did. I sent warm greetings. And what do I get back? Nothing. A big fat *nothing* from Private First Class Joe Berger of Biloxi, Mississippi. Pop says I have to be patient. YOUR PEN PAL IS FAR AWAY FROM HOME, JULIE. LETTERS TAKE A LONG TIME TO CROSS THE SEA. Too bad, manners are manners.

HOLDING A GRUDGE ISN'T NEARLY AS INTERESTING AS WRITING ANOTHER LETTER. That's another thing Pop says. He says it a lot. Even though I *don't* hold a grudge. I'm not that kind of person. And just to prove it, I write another letter, *warm greetings from the home front* and all that, and it's a really interesting letter. I sound *mature*. More like fourteen, maybe sixteen. I find a pretty picture. For Joe. And *autograph* it: *To Joe, With Affection From Your Pen Pal, Julie*. Then I go for a swim. Swim first. Take the letter to the post office later.

Well, that was the good part of the

story. Now comes the bad part. At approximately 3:00 that same afternoon, the afternoon of August 15 to be precise, Bruno — horrible, horrible Bruno — *reads my letter.* This is a true fact. I know it's a true fact because I actually catch him in the act. Now a lot of people would yell and scream if you read their personal letter, but not me. I just stick out my hand as if to say, PUT IT HERE, BUDDY. And he does. He puts the letter in my hand and that's when my picture slips out of the envelope and that horrible, horrible boy *grabs* it midair. He stares at the picture. Stares and stares and stares. Then he laughs.

It's like the end of the world when Bruno laughs at me.

I thought it was a good idea when I did it. When I cut out the picture of the girl in the magazine. And signed my name.

Honestly, I thought it was a good idea. *So what if it's not really me. She's so much prettier than me, and my soldier will think I'm pretty!* That's what I thought when I did it. I thought it was a good idea. But it was more like a *disaster.*

Martha

It's not fair. Because Julie won't let me *touch* her letters. Or *read* her letters. Or *watch* when she is writing her letters. NOT EVERYTHING IS YOUR BUSINESS, MARTHA. THIS ISN'T KID STUFF, MARTHA. MY SOLDIER IS AN IMPORTANT AIRMAN IN THE WAR, AND HE'S *EXPECTING* MY LETTER, MARTHA.

So what, all I did was borrow her dumb old letter. To read on the beach. I didn't know it was going to blow away! It wasn't supposed to blow away! But there goes Julie's letter . . . and you should see me running after Julie's letter! Which I finally caught and then I saw Bruno on the beach. LOOK WHAT I HAVE, BRUNO. YOU HAVE TO READ IT OUT LOUD, I said. IT'S IMPORTANT. He unfolds the letter . . . and *that's* when Julie showed up! Bruno was in *big trouble.*

Bruno

The letters stopped coming. Sometimes you got three in one day and other times you waited a whole week, but that summer, the summer we found the baby, the letters from Ben stopped coming. *Today,* you think, *today there's a letter, for sure.* You stand in line at the post office. It's a really long line, and the door is open but it's hot, really, really hot, and you wonder if every-one — all your Belle Beach neighbors — are thinking the same thing, *today's the day . . .* Days and weeks and nothing from Ben, not a word. And then, finally, it comes. A letter from Ben, and it's just for me, not my parents and me. The letter that would change our lives forever.

Speaking of letters, what do I care about Julie's letter to some soldier? I have more important things to think about. Tons of them, but try explaining that to Julie when she's *screaming her head off,* saying things like HOW COULD YOU! HOW DARE YOU! I HATE YOU! Technically, of course, it's all Martha's fault. She's the one who had me thinking the world comes to an end if we don't read that letter. And by the way, I didn't even know — not yet — that it was Julie who wrote it. Also by the way, there's something you should know about Martha. *She tells stories.* Pretty much all the time, and it's practically impossible to figure out which of them are real and which ones are made up. She's got this gravely little whispery voice, so you lean in when she talks, like everything is for your ears only. *Julie's pen pal is a famous airman in the war, he flies planes in the war!* True or made up? *My pop is friends with President Roosevelt!* True or made up? *Miss Bancroft is coming for dinner tonight and we're going to the movies tonight in her jeep!* True or made up?

I remember telling my mom, way back at the beginning of summer, YOU MIGHT BE INTERESTED TO KNOW THERE'S NO SIGN OF A MOM OVER THERE, AT THE COTTAGE NEXT DOOR. But she already knew about next door and told me the girls' mother had died a few years back. When she said it, her left eyebrow shot up. Mom's Warning Look, that's what you call that eyebrow thing, and this time she was warning me, *Be nice to those girls, Bruno. You better be nice to those girls.*

And I am. I'm very nice. So when Martha said we had to read some important letter, something to do with some soldier, my first thought was, *Okay, fine, let's read the letter.* My second thought was, *Hey, maybe this guy knows Ben!* Then all of a sudden Julie is there, grabbing the letter out of my hands, acting like I've committed a *murder.* I can't really tell you *what* she's saying, only that it's loud. And that picture? It doesn't take a genius to figure out it's not a picture of Julie, even though she's gone ahead and written her name on it, and the question is *why. Why* would she do something like that? One more reason I'll never understand girls.

14.

THE THING ABOUT SECRETS

Julie

I'm no thief. Obviously. But once, when I was six years old, I did *kind of* steal something. A tiny silver bracelet, I stole it right out of Pop's dresser drawer and put it in my own dresser drawer, with some rolled-up socks. I knew exactly what it was (my mother's baby bracelet), and I knew exactly what I was doing, and I never told anyone. Not even Pop. Years and years went by and I still never told. I love the secret of holding it whenever I want. And touching the seven letters that spell her name. I take it to school sometimes, and nobody knows. I brought it to Belle Beach, and nobody knew. On the morning of the library party, I tucked it in my pocket and nobody knew. I was all dressed up in a dress, not shorts. And by the end of the morning, the bracelet wasn't a secret anymore.

ELEANOR. WE'LL BE NAMING YOU ELEANOR. That's what I told the baby whenever we stopped to rest on the beach. Mostly we rested for Martha. I'M TIRED, JULIE. . , . MY LEGS HURT, JULIE. . . . I WANT POP, JULIE. LET'S BRING THE BABY TO POP. That basket weighed a ton, by the way. A baby *plus* a bag full of baby things, such as diapers, pajamas, two bottles of milk, the pink sundress — it all adds up to heavy. So I stopped whenever Martha needed to stop, put down the basket, and talked to my little Eleanor. We loved each other very much. One time when we stopped, I put my mother's bracelet on her wrist, and wouldn't you know, it fit her tiny wrist. It was perfect.

Then we saw George on the beach. And the car.

Martha

Bossy Julie got to carry the baby and she wouldn't let me carry the baby even for one little minute on the beach. YOU HAVE A VERY IMPORTANT JOB, MARTHA. YOU HAVE TO BE OUR *LOOKOUT*, LIKE A REALLY GOOD SPY. YOU HAVE TO MAKE SURE WE AREN'T BEING FOLLOWED. You want to know what I saw? Because I'll tell if you want. I saw *Bruno* on the beach and didn't tell Miss Bossy. And that girl. I saw her, too. And she was following Bruno! I *am* a good spy.

Bruno

Usually I don't have too many secrets. But that day, the day we found the baby, I was all jammed up with them. Because of Ben's letter. The one my parents didn't know about. To tell you the truth, I got all kinds of *sidetracked* due to finding the baby, and somewhere along the way just totally forgot about Ben and the news in that top-secret letter. *Tess and I got married.* That's what he wrote. Pretty big news, right? *We got married in New York, the Sunday before I shipped out, and don't tell Mom and Dad. Whatever you do, Bruno, don't tell anyone, not yet.* There was more. *I haven't gotten a letter from Tess in a really long time. I'm worried. Really worried and don't ask why. You'll know why soon enough but you have to find her right away (her boardinghouse is at 241 East 39th Street in the city). Find Tess and bring her home with you. Bring her to Belle Beach. Mom and Dad will understand, you'll see. I'm counting on you, Bruno.*

That's a lot of secrets in just one day.

15.

INSIDE AND OUT AT THE LIBRARY

Julie

May I offer you a piece of this fine cake, Mrs. Roosevelt? I baked it myself. It's your favorite. May I show you around the new children's library, Mrs. Roosevelt? I had actually practiced saying those words. All of them. Many times. But by the time we were halfway to town that morning, I was totally convinced I'd done all that baking for nothing. Convinced she had never gotten my beautiful invitation. Convinced she had better things to do. Bruno was right. *Bruno.* The most maddening boy on earth. I hadn't said a word to him in sixteen days, and why would I? *He read my personal letter.* And *laughed at me.* What could be worse than that? Nothing. That's what. Well, I took care of that picture, all right, and the letter. Tore them into a thousand pieces, that's what I did, and threw them in the ocean, goodbye. Which proves I'm a terrible pen pal after all.

The closer we got to town, the madder I got. Things kept popping into my head, and every single one of them made me *mad.* Including the fact that summer was nearly over. Just a few more days and we'd be going home. Did I want to go home? No. Not yet. I love my home and I love New York, but I wanted to stay here some more. Here in Belle Beach. WHY NOT? I said that to Pop. I said it a few times that week. The week before we found the baby. WHY CAN'T WE JUST LIVE IN BELLE BEACH FOR A WHILE? MARTHA AND I CAN GO

TO SCHOOL HERE, I said. THINK OF THE FRESH AIR! *BEACH* AIR, I said, IT'S GOOD FOR CHILDREN. AND YOU COULD WRITE ANOTHER BOOK HERE! IN THE FRESH AIR! Pop pretended to listen to my good ideas. YOU'RE RIGHT ABOUT ALL OF IT, he said. BUT I'M AFRAID IT'S NOT PRACTICAL, JULIE. MAYBE WE'LL COME BACK NEXT SUMMER, he said. And *then,* completely out of nowhere, the subject was, of all things, *Miss Bancroft.* SHE COMES TO THE CITY NOW AND THEN, AND MIGHT STOP BY TO SEE US SOMETIME. WHEN SHE'S IN THE CITY, he said. WELL, SHE CAN'T BE MY MOTHER IF THAT'S WHAT YOU'RE THINKING, I said, FORGET ABOUT THAT!

We were nearly there. Nearly at the library, and I didn't see anyone else on Main Street. Just me and Martha, and she was holding my hand. Martha loves to hold my hand. Hers is so little and warm. It's always warm, even in winter. I TOLD MRS. BEN-ELI TO GET READY FOR A BIG SURPRISE AND NOW THERE *IS* NO SURPRISE, NO ELEANOR ROOSEVELT. That's what I told Martha and I heard myself sigh. Martha patted my hand. DON'T WORRY, JULIE. SHE'LL BE HERE.

It was just after she said, DON'T WORRY, JULIE, SHE'LL BE HERE, that I saw the basket. And the baby inside.

Martha

Mrs. Ben-Eli said I would get *my own* library card! Right after the ribbon-cutting ceremony! I couldn't wait to have *my own* library card! You're allowed to borrow eight books at a time at the new children's library! POP, I said, YOU HAVE TO HELP ME FIND EIGHT BOOKS. THEY ALL START *"ONCE UPON A TIME."* AND THEY ALL END *"AND THEY ALL LIVED HAPPILY EVER AFTER."*

Bruno

That morning, the morning we found the baby, my mother was inside the library, putting the finishing touches on everything for the Grand Opening, making sure everything was perfect. My father was across the street at Ben-Eli's, setting up for the day. He made a sign to stick on the door. BEN-ELI'S CLOSED TODAY FROM 11 TO 2 FOR TOWN EVENT AT THE NEW CHILDREN'S LIBRARY! COME TO THE LIBRARY! SUPPORT YOUR TOWN! IT'S PATRIOTIC! I was supposed to be getting to the library at nine, to help out. That had been the plan. My mother's plan. But then Ben's letter came and I had to choose between my mother's plan (library) and Ben's (take the train to New York). Ben's plan was the winner. Only I never did make that 9:15 to the city.

16.

BREAD AND CHEESE AND BIG PURPLE PLUMS

Julie

I knew it the second I saw her. That second, I knew I was standing just a few feet away from *Eleanor Roosevelt*. Honestly, she was wearing these *awful* brown shoes. You know the kind, sturdy city shoes, and her feet were *sinking*. I swear they were sinking in the sand! Normally you would tell a person *barefoot is best on the beach! Just take off your shoes!* But of course you would never say such a thing to *Eleanor Roosevelt*. Unless you are Martha. Not only did she say it, she knew exactly who she was talking to, like this: YOU SHOULD TAKE OFF YOUR

SHOES, MRS. ROOSEVELT! THE SAND FEELS NICE. AND TICKLY IN YOUR TOES! Mrs. Roosevelt smiled at Martha. (Remember? Grown-ups *always* love Martha.) FRANKLY, she said, I'M NOT IN THE HABIT OF TAKING OFF MY SHOES IN PUBLIC. *She's here!* I kept saying it to myself. *She's here! She's here! She's here!* Martha was telling her everyone's name: I'M MARTHA ... THAT ONE IS JULIE ... But inside my head: *She's here! She's here!* Over and over again. Until I heard Martha say, NANCY. THIS IS OUR BABY SISTER, NANCY. At that point the only thing in my head was this: *My little sister is lying to Eleanor Roosevelt.*

Martha

We had a picnic with Mrs. Roosevelt!
Bread and cheese and big purple plums! I
hate cheese, so I took one purple plum and
said, THANK YOU, MRS. ROOSEVELT. Julie
took one purple plum. Bruno took a lot of
bread and cheese and two purple plums.
We found milk in the basket that came with
the baby, and guess who fed the baby? Mrs.
Roosevelt! She looked at Nancy's little
bracelet, and said, OH, WHAT A LOVELY
BRACELET . . . FANCY THAT, IT'S EVEN
ENGRAVED. George and I, we were wish-
ing Mrs. Roosevelt could be our grandma.

Bruno

So now I'm in the presence of Eleanor Roosevelt. Crazy, right? And I'm wondering how you tell Eleanor Roosevelt she's talking to a couple of *kidnappers,* and by the way, that baby on your lap, well, that happens to be *stolen goods.* Julie, meanwhile, is giving me her killer *you better keep your mouth shut* look. Which I completely ignore.

Okay, now picture this. We're all sitting around, eating this great food that just kind of appears out of nowhere, and the baby is falling asleep in Mrs. Roosevelt's lap and Mrs. Roosevelt says, real casual,

SO HOW OLD IS NANCY? It's a pretty easy question, right? No big deal. Only it kind of becomes a big deal and here's why: Martha, Julie, and I answer at the same exact time. Unfortunately, we all say something different. TWO YEARS OLD (Martha). FIVE DAYS OLD (Julie). TWO MONTHS OLD (me). Mrs. Roosevelt doesn't say a word. She just smiles at the baby and rubs her little wrist, the one with the bracelet.

All of a sudden I look at my watch. Ben's watch. *Ben.* The city. The train to New York. The 9:15 to the city. I missed that one all right, a long time ago. Next train, 11:15. Leave now. Run. Ben is counting on me. WELL, I HAVE TO GO SOMEWHERE. I stand up and that's when I see Tess. Ben's Tess. Running across the sand, arms flailing. Tess, running full speed ahead.

17.

TESS

Julie

I guess Mrs. Roosevelt is some kind of baby *expert*. She held the baby and fed the baby and burped the baby and sang. It was after the singing, that's when I saw the girl from the ice-cream shop. The girl who got on the train that day, she was running toward us, maybe shouting, maybe crying, and coming in for a landing on the big beach blanket. Arms, hands, reaching for the baby. MY BABY, she cried! I'M SORRY! SO SORRY! I'M HERE, EMMIE, HERE! MY BABY! I never saw anyone cry so hard.

Martha

We got to ride in the big black car with Mrs. Roosevelt! Mr. Hicks, the driver, took us all the way back to the library! Julie was so sad. It's because she wasn't holding the baby anymore. Tess was holding the baby. I LOVE YOU, I LOVE YOU, I LOVE YOU. Tess said that about two million times to the baby. YOU CAN CALL HER NANCY, I said.

Bruno

No way. No way was I getting in the car with them. I had to run. Had to get there first. Me, I was the one who had to break the news. So I ran my fastest — probably broke some record — all the way to the library. A lot of people were waiting outside. More than a lot. The whole town, I think, maybe the *world*. There was a long red ribbon and my mom was on the top step, and my dad was there, next to Mom. I looked at my watch. Ben's watch. Nearly eleven. Nearly time for the Grand

Opening, which my parents kept saying was not only a small-town event, but a *patriotic* one as well. MOM! I called. MOM! She couldn't hear, so I called louder. DAD! I called. HEY, DAD! I squeezed through the crowd, to the top of the steps.

My mom knew. I knew she knew the minute she saw me. My mom's like that. She knows if you leave your homework for the last minute even though you'd never announce that kind of thing, and she knows if you don't make your bed even if she's downstairs and your bed is upstairs, and she knows if you hit a ball through someone's living-room window by mistake. That morning, she took one look at me. And knew.

The big car rolled up to the library and stopped in front of the sign that said NO PARKING TODAY! BIG CELEBRATION TODAY! The back door opened. Martha got out, then Julie. Then Tess and the baby in her arms and Eleanor Roosevelt. *MOM, I whispered. HEY, MOM, HEY, DAD. SOME-BODY WANTS TO MEET YOU.*

18.

WHAT-IFS

Julie

Sometimes I think, what if I didn't see the
basket? BUT YOU DID, Pop said. He said it
that night. After Martha went to sleep and
George went to sleep, and we were sitting
on the porch watching the night. Just me
and Pop, and that's when he said, LUCK,
JULIE. SOMETIMES, WHEN WE LEAST
EXPECT IT, IT JUST SHOWS UP. TODAY,
FOR EXAMPLE, RIGHT HERE IN BELLE
BEACH, A HEAP OF GOOD LUCK, WHEN
YOU FOUND THE BABY.

Martha

What if we couldn't find Julie's cake?
But we did! We found it *inside* the library
and Mrs. Roosevelt ate a big fat piece
of Julie's cake! MMMMNNN, she said.
MMMNNN. Pop took forty million
pictures all day! Julie and the baby.
Julie and Mrs. Roosevelt. Julie and Mrs.
Ben-Eli and Tess and the baby. Bruno and
Mr. Ben-Eli. Bruno and the baby. Bruno
and Mrs. Ben-Eli and Mr. Ben-Eli and
Tess and the baby. George and the baby.
George and me and the baby. WE'RE

SENDING THESE TO BEN, Pop said. A GREAT BIG POUCH FULL OF PICTURES, JUST WAIT TILL HE SEES WHAT'S WAITING FOR HIM!

Bruno

What might have made sense, when we found her, was to take the baby *into* the library since my mother was inside, setting things up for the party. If there's anyone who would know what to do with a baby in a basket, it's my mom. I never even thought of it, though.

According to my parents, the Grand Opening was a huge success. Books. Library cards. A couple of medium-boring speeches and thank-yous to the Good Ladies, and believe it or not, there was even *dancing* in the library. Mrs. Roosevelt

didn't do any dancing, by the way, and nei-
ther did I. Kevin was dancing all over the
place. With something like six different
girls, but once I saw him dancing with his
mother. Paul's mother. Well, you never
saw so many people in such a good mood.
At least not since the war started. And all
those good-mood people would go home
later, and write to their soldiers overseas,
and tell them about this day in August in
the little seaside town of Belle Beach. WE
HAVE TO SHARE THIS WITH OUR BOYS
OVER THERE, OUR HEROES, AND LET
THEM KNOW *ALL THIS IS WAITING FOR
YOU. WE'RE ALL JUST WAITING FOR YOU
TO COME HOME.* My father told me that.

19.

THINGS YOU DON'T NECESSARILY TELL

Julie

Bruno thinks he's this great *detective* or something, but he's not. I knew he was following me! Of course I knew! I just ignored him, that's all. We weren't exactly on speaking terms. But he wouldn't go away.

I had to save the baby. She was *my* responsibility. I've always been kind of mature for my age, and maybe I'm too serious. Sometimes I wish I had a silly side to me, but I'm just not made that way. ON THE BRIGHT SIDE, ONLY SOMEONE WITH A SERIOUS SIDE WOULD HAVE KNOWN

EXACTLY WHAT TO DO WITH THE BABY.
Pop told me that. Silly wouldn't get the job
done.

It's true I wanted to keep her. I wanted it
more than anything. But I would never do
that. Tess is her mother, not me. Beautiful
Tess.

Martha

The baby has brown curly hair. My hair is straight. It is dark brown and my eyes are dark brown. I looked, but the baby has no freckles. I looked hard, but not even one. I have a bunch, but just on my nose. I hope she gets freckles and looks like me. Everyone is always saying, OH, THAT JULIE LOOKS JUST LIKE HER MOTHER. They never say it about me.

Bruno

I saw Tess that morning. Or at least I *thought* I saw Tess that morning. It was really early, right when I got to the library. I saw her behind the green bench. Or maybe she was *on* the green bench, who can remember. *Hey Tess! I thought you were in New York . . . Ben said to find you in New York . . .* I would have said all that, but then everything was happening with the baby and I guess I forgot. Forgot about Tess. Until I was out there on the beach, and I turned around once, and thought I saw her again. Following me. Following the baby.

20.

THE THING ABOUT FRIENDS

Julie

Okay, fine. I had to start talking to Bruno again. How could I not? It happened late that afternoon. After the library party. After Tess and the baby went home to the Ben-Elis'. Bruno found me on the beach, and just like that, we were talking again. I told him it was probably against the law, reading someone's letter. IF I WERE A DIFFERENT KIND OF PERSON, I'D REPORT YOU, BRUNO. TO THE POLICE! Then he said, YOU KNOW ABOUT *KIDNAPPING*, RIGHT? YOU SHOULD KNOW IT'S A CRIMINAL ACT. NO TWO WAYS ABOUT

IT. I told him I'm no *criminal*. I was doing a good deed. Taking her to Camp Mitchel, to the nurses there, and they would help me find her mother. CRIMINAL ACT, he said. NOT, I said. Then one of us — can't remember which one — said maybe we shouldn't talk about it anymore. And we didn't.

Bruno pulled this wrinkled envelope out of his pocket. BABY INSTRUCTIONS, he said. THEY CAME IN THE BASKET WITH THE BABY, REMEMBER? WE'RE A LITTLE LATE, BUT WANT TO LOOK? Did I ever! So we sat on the beach and read the instructions.

Her name is Emmie Louise Ben-Eli.
She is two months old. She is perfect.
Please take her into the library. Now!
As soon as you find her, take her
inside. Ask for Mrs. Ben-Eli. Only
Mrs. Ben-Eli. *When she sees*

Emmie, she will know. And reach for
her granddaughter. She will know this
is Ben's baby, and mine. I can't do this
alone. Emmie needs her grandparents.
Her family. And I need them, too.
Please bring the baby inside. To Mrs.
Ben-Eli. I'll be waiting. Right here. On
the green bench.

With thanks from Tess Ben-Eli

We sat there for a long time. And didn't
say a word.

Martha

Once Bruno threw a baseball. High! Over the ocean! *CATCH, BEN!* That's what he said when he was throwing the ball. ARE YOU THROWING IT TO BEN? I said. Bruno got mad. YOU ARE WAY TOO NOSY, he said. COME ON, GEORGE, I said. LET'S GO *HOME.* I was mad at Bruno. But the next day I wasn't mad anymore. Because Bruno is my friend.

Bruno

Julie's the one who said it first. UNCLE
BRUNO. She said it all serious and Julie-
like. YOU'RE AN ACTUAL *UNCLE,* BRUNO!
And I am. Uncle Bruno! Not bad, right? I'm
going to write Ben tonight. Second time in
a week. Usually you'll never catch me writing twice in a week. But I figure he'll want
to hear all about how we found the baby.
We found Tess, too, and Tess found us, and
now there are two extra people living in
the house. *And by the way,* I'll say, *Mom and
Dad keep picking up the baby, even when she's
sleeping. They walk around the house holding*

on to Emmie like they'll never let go. I have to come up with a good joke, too. For Ben. *And by the way,* I'll say, *the summer people are getting ready to leave. Even the good ones . . . but hey, sometimes you get lucky and the good ones come back.*

And before I sign off, I'll tell him the main thing. Which is this.

Come on home, Ben, we're waiting.